CIRCLE OF THREE

Enough Friendship to Go Around?

written by Elizabeth Brokamp

illustrated by Joni Stringfield

MAGINATION PRESS • WASHINGTON, D.C.

For Robert, who always believes — EB

To Dad and Mom, the best parents a girl could have — JS

Published by
MAGINATION PRESS
An Educational Publishing Foundation Book
American Psychological Association
750 First Street, NE
Washington, DC 20002

For more information about our books, including a complete catalog, please write to us, call 1-800-374-2721, or visit our website at www.maginationpress.com.

Editor: Darcie Conner Johnston
Art Director: Susan K. White
Project Coordinator: Becky Shaw

Library of Congress Cataloging-in-Publication Data

Brokamp, Elizabeth.
Circle of three : enough friendship to go around? / written by Elizabeth Brokamp ; illustrated by Joni Stringfield.
p.   cm.
Summary: Fifth-graders Lindsey, Bella, and Kate, who have been best friends forever, deal with new feelings as they expand their social circle and find interests that threaten their comfortable relationship. Includes discussion questions at the end of each chapter.
ISBN-13: 978-1-4338-0321-5 (hardcover : alk. paper)
ISBN-10: 1-4338-0321-6 (hardcover : alk. paper)
ISBN-13: 978-1-4338-0322-2 (pbk. : alk. paper)
ISBN-10: 1-4338-0322-4 (pbk. : alk. paper)
[1. Best friends—Fiction. 2. Friendship—Fiction.] I. Stringfield, Joni, ill. II. Title.
PZ7.B7863Ci 2008
[Fic]—dc22   2007046476

Manufactured in the United States of America
10 9 8 7 6 5 4 3 2 1

Good things come in threes.

That's what my mom always says when Kate, Bella, and I walk in the door.

And mostly it's true. Three friends can play most board games, jump rope together, invent a club, play hide-and-seek, start an all-girl band, build an awesome fort, have laughing fits, and do a really good dance routine.

But three doesn't always feel so fun. When there are three friends, somewhere, sometime, somehow, someone is going to feel left out...

Chapter 1

Three means if the teacher

asks you to pick partners,

it's a race to see who can catch eyes first.

"**E**verybody ready?" Bella asked.

"Ready!" said Kate.

"Ready!" I shouted.

When you have two best friends, there's no such thing as opening your new homeroom assignments alone. Summer was almost over, and the three of us were squeezed into Kate's hammock, getting excited about fifth grade, and getting nervous, too. Would we be in the same class this year? We held our breaths and our big manila school envelopes, waiting for the ready-set-go to tear them open.

"Let her rip!" Bella pinched her eyes shut and yanked the flap off. "Ogden!" she screamed.

"Ogden! Me, too!" Kate whooped, waving her letter around in the air.

"I can't get this thing out of here," I wailed, tugging at the paper. It was stuck in the envelope like gum to the bottom of a desk.

"Hurry, Lindsey! What's it say?"

Finally I tore it out in about eight pieces. But I could still see which teacher I got. "Oh, man," I groaned.

"Oh, no," said Bella.

"What? What?" asked Kate in a squeaky voice.

I tried to look the way I felt when I thought Harry Potter was dead, but couldn't keep it up. "Ogden!" I burst out laughing. "I got Ogden, too! That makes all three of us!"

"Oh, my gosh! Really? Really?" Bella swung the hammock so hard we almost fell out.

"We can do the Egypt project together!"

"And study for all our tests and quizzes!"

"And Kate, you can tutor Bella and me in math!"

"Lindsey can make sure we don't flunk language arts!"

"And Bella can help us with science!" (Bella's going to be a famous scientist some day, I can just tell. She'll probably discover life on another planet or something.)

"Yeah, between us we have a study group for everything," said Kate. "Oh, you guys. This is going to be so cool!"

And it was totally cool. Until it wasn't.

"For our first project of the year, we'll be working in partners," Mr. Ogden said. "Time now to choose. Pick carefully. Your grade will depend on participation and both people's contributions."

Bella and I grabbed hands. Mr. Ogden seated us by alphabetical order, and our last names—Ming and McCann—meant we were right next to each other. We looked back at Kate, stuck in the Z's. She gave us a look that would say "save me, *pleeeease*" if it could talk.

"Mr. Ogden?" I raised my hand.

"Yes, Miss McCann?"

"Can we have a group of three? It looks like we have an odd number of people, so it would make sense," I said hopefully.

"Partners, as in two people, Miss McCann. We have a new student joining our class tomorrow, and whoever doesn't have a partner today will find him or herself paired up then."

"Uh, okay," I said. "Sorry!" I mouthed to Kate.

"She looks crushed," Bella whispered, "totally and completely crushed."

"Yeah, Mr. Ogden is so mean. Is this what it's going to be like every time we do a project?" I was starting to wish I lived in Alaska, where the teachers are probably never so picky and strict.

"Probably. What can we do? It's kind of not fair that we get to be partners all year just because we're M's."

"We could maybe make a schedule."

"Just take turns, you mean?"

"Yeah, next time you can be her partner. Then I can be." We looked over at Kate. She was working with Brian Young, the official class goofball, and looking like she'd just eaten moldy bread.

"For sure!" we both said at the same time.

It made me feel better, figuring out how to fix the problem. I mean, I don't exactly want to be the one without a partner, but it wouldn't be fair if Kate always had to be the one, just because of the alphabet. Best friends don't do that.

"Let's tell Kate our plan at lunch. We can map out who's doing what," I said.

"Okay. Uh-oh, here comes Ogden. Look busy."

When the lunch bell rang, we picked up our stuff and waited for Kate. She came out with her head down. "Hi," I said, and gave her a hug.

"Was it terrible working with Brian? Like someone was poking needles under your fingernails?" asked Bella. "Like a cobra was eating your toes?"

"Like your nose hairs were getting pulled out one by one?" I added.

Kate finally smiled. "Well, maybe not quite that bad."

"Hey, we're making a schedule for projects, if it's okay with you. Next time we pick partners, Lindsey said she'll find another partner so you and I can work together."

"Really?" she said, looking back and forth at us.

"Yeah, really."

"You guys are the best!"

BFF! (That means Best Friends Forever.) We walked arm-in-arm-in-arm to the lunchroom.

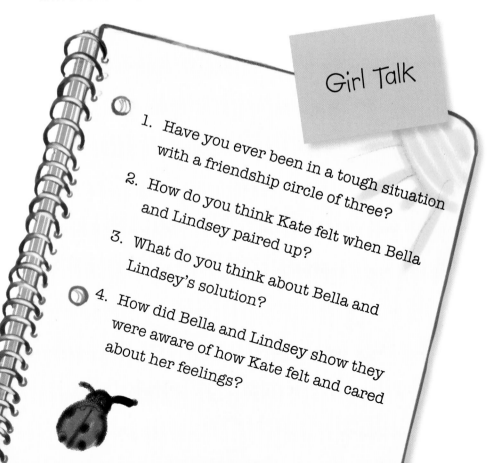

Girl Talk

1. Have you ever been in a tough situation with a friendship circle of three?

2. How do you think Kate felt when Bella and Lindsey paired up?

3. What do you think about Bella and Lindsey's solution?

4. How did Bella and Lindsey show they were aware of how Kate felt and cared about her feelings?

Chapter 2

Three means if your mom says
only one person can spend the night,
you're stuck making a hard choice.

"**H**ey Mom?** Since Jake's having someone over tomorrow night, can I, too?"

"I guess that will be all right. Your dad and I invited the Gardeners over for dinner, though, so you kids will have to remember to keep it down."

"Okay. Can I ask both Bella and Kate?"

"Oh, honey, I don't think so. Not this time. Don't you and Bella have your dance audition to prepare for? Maybe just ask her this time."

"But, Mom, Kate will be crushed if we leave her out again. Bella and I are already paired up for Mr. Ogden's history project." Maybe if I really begged she would soften up. "Please? Pretty please?"

"Lindsey, I don't think any one of you should expect to always do things as a threesome. It's just not practical. You can invite Kate next time." There's this tone my mom's voice gets sometimes, and it means "discussion over." This was it.

I called Bella. "So do you want to come over tomorrow night for a sleepover? My mom already said it was okay. Plus Jake is having Brian Windsor over. We can watch scary movies with them."

"What did Kate say?" Bella asked.

"I can't invite her. I'm only allowed to have one person. I thought we could practice our audition routines, too."

Bella let out a long, low whistle.

"I know, I know," I said. "It really stinks, but I mean, come on, it's not like we can do things in threes all the time, you know? Especially if our parents make dumb rules about it."

"Sort of," Bella said. "But I'm pretty sure she won't see it that way. So how are you going to break the news?"

"Well, I kind of thought we wouldn't. You know, a 'don't ask, don't tell' kind of thing. She doesn't have to know we're leaving her out. After all, we do have to practice for the audition. It's not like she even takes dance."

"Oh, Lindsey, I don't think that will work. I mean, do you think all day at school tomorrow she's not going to ask at least one of us what we're doing on Friday night? You should just tell her and get it over with."

"Then I think you should tell her. I mean, you can explain that it's not me, it's my mom. You can be like, 'Lindsey is so mad at her mom.'"

"Oh, peachy," Bella said. She sounded about as excited as my dad when my mom makes him take her to the opera.

"Please? You can make it sound a lot nicer than I can."

"Nice? I can't work miracles. 'Hello, Kate? Your two best friends are planning a sleepover without you, but don't feel left out or anything, because you're not. Well, you kind of are, but we don't want you to feel lousy about it, okay?' Great."

"Maybe don't say that part," I said. "Just blame it on my mom. It's her fault anyway."

"Okay," Bella said. "But for doing your dirty work, I will be expecting lots of chocolate chip cookies at your house tomorrow."

"I'll get right on it." I was so relieved I would have even cleaned out her locker for a week. (They could film a horror movie in Bella's locker.) "Um, call her tonight, okay? Then call me back?"

Bella sighed. "Might as well get it over with. If you don't hear from me before bed, call 9-1-1."

Ten minutes later, the phone rang. "Weird, weird, weird," Bella said.

"Uh-oh. What does that mean? She was really wigged out, huh?"

"Actually, I'm way more wigged out than she is. Get this. She'd already made plans with Hailey for tomorrow night."

"Hailey, the new girl? The one who came here from England?"

"Yep. Kate said she's really cool but she doesn't have many friends yet. They're going to Kate's riding lesson after school. Then Kate's dad is taking them to a movie."

"Oh. Well, maybe she's so mad she made it all up."

"I don't think so. Her exact words were, 'Phew, I'm so relieved. I was worried you guys would be mad at me for having her over without you,' or something like that. I could hear her chewing on her braid. You know how she does that when she's nervous about something."

"Oh." I was quiet.

"Yeah. I think we just got dissed in reverse."

I pictured Kate chewing on her braid, and had to laugh. "Well, maybe not," I said. "I mean, we were basically going to do the same thing to her. You know Kate. She's being sweet and making sure the new girl has friends. That's one of the things we love about her."

"Yeah, I guess so," Bella admitted.

"So I owe you some cookies. Chocolate chip, right?"

"Definitely. 'Night, Linds."

14

Girl Talk

1. What do you think about how Lindsey and Bella handled this situation? How about Kate?

2. What mix of feelings do you think Bella and Lindsey might be experiencing?

3. Lindsey doesn't entirely agree with Bella that Kate has "dissed" them. What do you think would have happened if Lindsey had agreed with Bella? How would things have turned out differently?

4. Which sentence do you agree with most:
   a. My feelings hit me like a freight train. My body sends them, and I don't have any control over when or why.
   b. I have a choice about how I feel. If I change my thoughts, I can change my feelings sometimes, too.
   c. Other people make me feel things. It's all their fault.

   What are the pros and cons of believing the way you do? Which belief makes you feel the most powerful? Which one makes you feel the most helpless?

5. Why would Lindsey's mom say that it's not always practical to do things as a threesome? Do you agree?

Chapter 3

Three means if you have a fight,
one friend
usually gets stuck in the middle.

TGIF! Thank goodness it's Friday!

Fridays at our school are awesome because it's (1) pizza day, (2) almost the weekend, (3) time for free play in gym, and (4) almost the weekend. (Did I say that one already?) Plus I'm especially psyched today because Kate and Bella and I are supposed to go bowling tonight with some kids from Bella's swim team. I'm not wild about bowling usually, but Lanes of America paints the bowling balls in neon colors, and then they turn off all the lights on Friday night and play crazy music. Everything glows in the dark, and it's really fun.

I was practically skipping on my way to the bus stop. (I mean, I would have been skipping if I were a little kid.) "Hey, guys! Woo-hoo, neon bowling night! We should wear white so we glow, too."

I stopped and looked from Kate to Bella. "What? Did somebody die or something? Oh, no, Kate. It wasn't Harry, was it?" Kate's guinea pig had been making weird rasping noises for a week.

"Ask her," Kate said, pointing toward Bella but without looking at her.

Uh-oh. I looked at Bella. "It's not Harry?"

"No, it's not the stupid guinea pig," Bella said. "She's mad because I told my mom that she never really cleans her room when her mom says. She just shoves stuff in the closet and then tells her mom 'All done!' and collects her allowance."

"Harry's not stupid," Kate said hotly. "And I got in trouble because of what Bella said. She's not telling everything either. Ask her about the toothbrush."

I looked from one to the other. "The toothbrush?" I said to Bella.

"I might have mentioned that Kate runs the water for a few minutes extra after she finishes brushing her teeth so her mom doesn't bug her about getting cavities."

"And the junk food?" Kate snapped.

Bella answered, "Well, so? Kate keeps junk food in her desk. So when her mom says she can't have any more, she can just get some from her room."

I looked at Bella. "You told your mom all that stuff?"

"What?" she said, raising her hands like this was a stick-up. "I mean, it's not like I told about her secret crush or something. Besides, I didn't think my mom would say anything."

Kate snorted.

Bella crossed her arms and looked at me. "You tell her that if she just did what her mom said, there wouldn't be anything to get in trouble for in the first place."

Kate kicked the ground. "Tell her that good friends don't rat on each other, but I guess since she's not a good friend she wouldn't know that." She stormed off in the direction of the bus shelter.

Bella and I stood there.

"Uh," I said. "So are we still going bowling?"

"I'm still going, but she's not. How about you? Are you coming with us?"

"Um, I'm not sure, I guess. I mean, it was supposed to be the three of us. It'll feel kind of weird going without Kate."

"I won't feel weird at all," Bella said. "She's being too sensitive. I mean, it's not like I have total control over my mother."

"Well, yeah," I said. "But, I mean, your mom and her mom are good friends. Didn't you sort of know that what you were saying could get her in trouble?"

"Whose side are you on?" Bella demanded.

"I'm not on any side. I just want to go bowling like we planned."

"Great," Bella said. "You know what? Let's just skip the bowling. I'll go with the swim team by myself." I watched her storm off in the direction of the stop sign.

Okay. Well. Maybe I would have better luck with Kate. "Hey," I said, as I walked over to the bus shelter.

"Hey," she said, her voice as flat as a pancake.

"So," I said. "So maybe Bella didn't mean all that stuff in a mean way? Maybe she was just kind of talking to her mom and it slipped out."

"Like calling Harry stupid?"

"Well, no," I said, starting to wish I lived someplace else, like Hawaii, where friends are probably never so unreasonable. "She's just mad. She didn't mean it. Can you just forgive her?"

Kate scuffed the ground with her shoes. "I can't trust her not to say stuff about me to her mom, she got me in trouble, she called my guinea pig stupid, and she ruined our plans for the weekend. Why would I forgive her? Whose side are you on anyway?"

I sighed. When would the school bus ever get here?

On the bus, the two of them sat far apart, Kate in the back, Bella in the front. I sat exactly in the middle. For the rest of the morning, they wouldn't speak to each other. They just kept telling me to tell the other person something.

By lunch, I was totally and completely fed up. I called the two of them together in the cafeteria. "Look," I said, furious. "Be mad at each other if you want, but I'm not going to get stuck in the middle anymore. I think both of you are acting like creeps, if you want to know the truth. I don't know who was more right or more wrong. What I know is that this stupid fight is ruining Friday and all the fun stuff we're supposed to be doing. And you know what? That stinks." This time I was the one who stormed away, leaving both of them standing there with their trays.

TBIF. (Too bad it's Friday.)

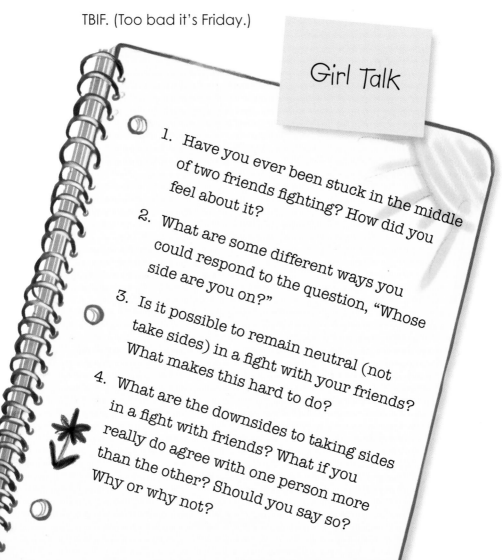

Girl Talk

1. Have you ever been stuck in the middle of two friends fighting? How did you feel about it?

2. What are some different ways you could respond to the question, "Whose side are you on?"

3. Is it possible to remain neutral (not take sides) in a fight with your friends? What makes this hard to do?

4. What are the downsides to taking sides in a fight with friends? What if you really do agree with one person more than the other? Should you say so? Why or why not?

Chapter 4

Three sometimes means

two against one.

"Chicken teri-yucky. Gross."

I set my tray on the table next to Kate's and Bella's lunchboxes, and hoped they would take pity on a starving BF. "Hey, guys, want to go to Monroe Street after school? We could walk over there and get a soda or something."

"Oh, you don't want to do that. I mean, I can't," Kate said quickly. "I have to, um, I mean, my mom needs me at home." She pulled her sandwich out of the plastic baggie and took a big bite.

"Okay," I said. "Bell, how about you?"

"Me neither, Linds. I have an appointment."

"Dentist again? I hate it when they do that fluoride thing. Doesn't it make you want to barf?"

"Not exactly the dentist," Bella said. "I forget what it is exactly. I just know I have something." She pulled her thermos out and began to pour her drink. The way she was concentrating on that drink, you'd think it was the most fascinating thing in the world.

"Well, okay. Maybe tomorrow, if you guys aren't busy then, too."

"Uh, sure. I mean, maybe," Kate said.

"I'll ask," Bella promised, shooting a look at Kate.

I picked at some rice with my fork. "So...what's happening with the slumber party? Anything new?" I asked. We'd been bugging our moms for weeks to let us have one.

"No, nothing," Kate said. "And nothing new with you either, Bella, right?"

"Nada," Bella said.

Something was weird. "Guys, is there something wrong? Did I do something that made you mad at me?"

"No, no," Bella protested. "We're all fine. Just tired."

I looked at Kate. "What?" she asked. "Oh. No, I'm not mad at you either."

"Well, okay, then." I took a bite of my dessert (if you can call old brown apple wedges dessert). We passed the last few minutes of lunch in silence.

It was when I was rounding the corner onto Monroe Street after school that I saw them: Kate and Bella, sitting at the counter, eating ice cream at The Scoop. I stood for a few seconds and stared, trying to figure out what to do. Then Kate looked up. "Oh, my gosh," I saw her gasp as she nudged Bella.

I burst into tears and ran the rest of the way home.

I cried all night in my room. Mom kept knocking and asking, "Bella's on the phone. You want to talk?" or "It's Kate. She'd like to say hi." But I wouldn't answer. How could they do this to me? I wish I'd never gotten up today. I wish I could move somewhere like Mexico, where people are probably never, ever this lousy to their friends.

The next day I said I didn't feel well, and my mom let me stay home. But the second day she said, "Lindsey, you can't run away from friend problems. You need to go back to school and deal with it. Work it out, honey." So I had to get dressed and figure out how to act normal after losing all the friends I had in the world.

The worst part was walking into class. I could feel the two of them staring at me and whispering. I went and sat with Charlie Grayson, the class nose-picker. Even being gross was better than being a back-stabber.

It was lunch when they cornered me. "You have to let

us explain," Kate said.

"Explain what exactly?" I asked in my snottiest voice. "How the two of you lied about what you were doing after school? How you totally left me out?" My eyes started to water. I couldn't help it.

"It's not like we wanted to lie to you," Bella said.

"We just didn't want to hurt your feelings," said Kate.

"Too late," I sniffed.

They just stood there, acting like they didn't know what else to say.

"So are you guys best friends without me now or something? What's the deal? Why are you being so mean? What did I ever do?"

"It wasn't about being mean, not at all. Our dads took us to the stadium for the baseball season opener, okay?"

"Yeah, they wanted to pick us up at school, but we told them no way. We didn't want you to feel left out. We asked them to pick us up at The Scoop instead, so it wouldn't hurt your feelings."

I couldn't believe this. "So, let me get this straight. You lied and went to get ice cream together to save my feelings?"

"Well, yeah, if you have to put it that way," Bella said.

Kate chimed in. "It wasn't even our idea to go to the game in the first place. Honest. Our dads were going. Probably it was our moms' idea to take us."

"Okay, you guys, can you see that this is kind of messed up? I think it's really lame that you wouldn't even tell me what you were doing."

Bella looked exasperated. "I'm sorry, but I mean, either way, you'd be mad, right? What exactly were we supposed to do?"

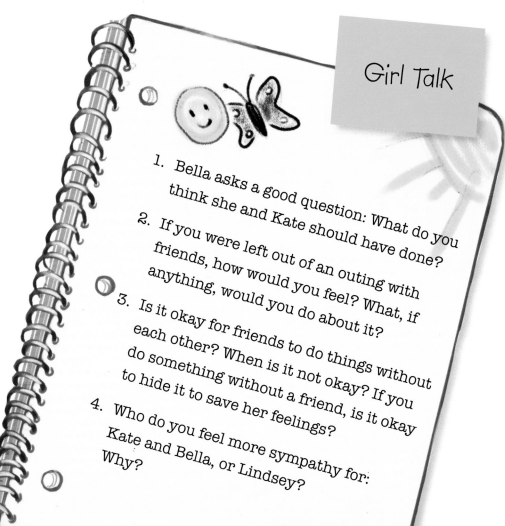

Girl Talk

1. Bella asks a good question: What do you think she and Kate should have done?

2. If you were left out of an outing with friends, how would you feel? What, if anything, would you do about it?

3. Is it okay for friends to do things without each other? When is it not okay? If you do something without a friend, is it okay to hide it to save her feelings?

4. Who do you feel more sympathy for: Kate and Bella, or Lindsey? Why?

Chapter 5

Three can be a really odd number.

Have you ever watched one of your best friends get stolen right out from under your nose? Let me tell you, it's no fun.

"What's up, Linds?" my mom asked, brushing out my hair. "You seem preoccupied. Is something wrong?"

"Not really," I said. "Not unless you call someone trying to steal your best friend a problem. Ow!" I yelled. My mom isn't exactly gentle with the tangles.

"Your hair's like a rat's nest underneath. Sit still, please. So who's trying to steal whom?"

"This new girl Hailey is trying to steal Kate away from me and Bella. She's, like, charming her to death with her British accent. And plus they're partners for our first project in Ogden's class and on the same soccer team together, so it's not like we can just, you know, charm her back."

"Are you sure this new girl is stealing Kate? Isn't it possible they're just becoming friends? You wouldn't want Kate not to have friends on her soccer team, would you?"

"Well, no, I guess not. But...oh, you wouldn't understand. It's just the way Hailey is doing it. She just walked right in and took Kate out from under us."

"Honey, you're talking about Kate like she's a pet or a favorite outfit. Hailey couldn't *take* her. Maybe they're just becoming friends. You know how it is when you have a new friend. You want to spend a lot of time together. But that newness will wear off, and Kate will still be your friend. My advice is, don't make a big deal out of it. Just let it go for now and see what happens."

"Are we done here?" I sighed. My mom clearly didn't get the social situation in fifth grade. We couldn't just do nothing while a friend-thief carted off Kate.

I called Bella. "Any good ideas yet?"

"Not too much. Get this. I talked to my dad about it, and you want to know what he said?"

"Let me guess. 'Don't do anything.' That was my mom's brilliant advice."

"Close. He said we should try to make friends with Hailey, and then all of us can be friends together. As if!"

"Yeah, it's like parents don't really get it. Anyway, I think I came up with something. We should just make Kate choose: Hailey or us. Simple."

"Hey, yeah! Totally brilliant!" Bella said, imitating Hailey's accent.

We laughed. Then Bella's voice went all serious. "Um, wait a sec. What if she picks Hailey?"

"You know she's going to choose us. We've been best friends for almost forever. Plus it will send a definite message to Hailey when Kate dumps her. 'Back off.' I like it." My sheer geniusness on this one made me proud.

"Great," Bella agreed. We'll meet her at the bus stop tomorrow morning and tell her then, okay?"

Bella and I hung up, happy to finally have a plan. If all went well, we'd be back to normal by first bell.

I was in a good mood when I woke up. My dad was always saying how important it is to take charge and stick up for yourself, and I think he has a point. Doing something is way better than doing nothing.

Kate and Bella were already at the bus stop when I got there. "So did you ask?" I said to Bella. Bella shook her head.

"Ask what?" Kate said.

"Um, well," I said, not sure how to start. "Here's the deal. We've kind of been talking, and we think it's really lousy how you're with Hailey so much these days. So, uh, we wanted to say that, well, you need to choose. Her or us." I exhaled.

"Oh, really," Kate said. "Is this your idea, too?" she asked Bella.

Bella nodded, looking less sure about it now.

"Great. Easy enough then," Kate said, her voice sounding super cheerful.

"Phew, we thought so," I said, relieved.

"If I have to choose,

I choose Hailey." Suddenly her voice was totally the opposite of cheerful. "She would never ask me to ditch my other friends. Thanks a lot."

Bella and I watched her board the bus without looking back, not even once.

That night, I didn't feel much like eating. When my mom asked me what was wrong, I said I was tired and went to bed early. She came into my room to say goodnight, and I started to cry. "Lindsey, honey, what's wrong, sweetheart?" My mom hugged me and waited for me to talk.

"It's just that everything's changed," I blurted out. "Things were great with my friends last year, and now it's all wrong, and it's Hailey's fault, only now it's really bad because everyone else in fifth grade likes her."

"Wait a minute, honey, slow down. Tell me from the very beginning."

"Well, remember how I told you about Hailey stealing Kate from us? You said Kate wasn't a thing and so she couldn't be stolen, but that's not true. Hailey has stolen the whole fifth grade basically. It was supposed to be our year, and now it's hers."

My mom was quiet a minute. "I think," she said slowly, "that this is one of those times you just have to live through. I could tell you all day long that things are going to work out just fine, but you wouldn't believe me, would you?"

I shook my head.

"Well, I can almost promise it will be okay. It will just take time. But you'll have to see that for yourself," my mom said, smiling. It was a nice smile, the kind of momly smile that makes you feel a little better, even if you are losing your best friend. She pulled the covers up, gave me a little kiss, and turned off the light.

1. What do you think about Bella and Lindsey's plan to ask Kate to choose between them and Hailey?

2. How do you think Kate felt when they asked her to make the choice?

3. How would you describe Lindsey's and Bella's feelings about Hailey? What advice would you give them about how to handle those feelings?

4. Lindsey thinks she is "sticking up for herself" by asking Kate to choose. Do you agree? Why or why not?

5. In conflicts with friends, do you agree with Lindsey that doing something is always better than doing nothing? Why or why not?

6. Lindsey's mom seems to think things will get better with time. Do you agree? How could time help?

Chapter 6

Three can feel like two too many

when you're mad.

Dear Diary:

Ask me yesterday, and I would have said I had two best friends. Today I think I have no friends in the world. Well, half a friend maybe, because Fiona stuck up for me. But she doesn't get full credit, because it's not like we hang out outside of school or anything.

This is going to sound really dumb, I know, but it started over a stupid magazine that Kate's mom gave her. Kate and Bella were sitting together and looking at the pictures, laughing about them.

"Hey, guys," I said. "What's so funny?"

They looked at each other and laughed some more, but nobody said anything.

I asked again. "Let me see. What's in there?"

More laughing. I started to get annoyed, especially because now Kate was practically falling out of her chair.

"Fine. Don't tell me," I said, and started to walk away.

"Hold on, Lindsey. Don't be like that," Bella said, giggling. "It's just that you're not going to think it's funny."

"Yeah, Lindsey. It's just, oh, how shall I say it? Too mature for you. You wouldn't get it."

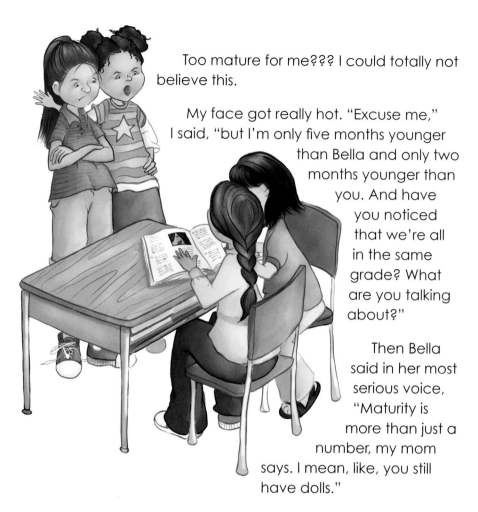

Too mature for me??? I could totally not believe this.

My face got really hot. "Excuse me," I said, "but I'm only five months younger than Bella and only two months younger than you. And have you noticed that we're all in the same grade? What are you talking about?"

Then Bella said in her most serious voice, "Maturity is more than just a number, my mom says. I mean, like, you still have dolls."

"Don't go there," Kate warned.

"Yeah, and you still bring the stuffed animal you had when you were two years old to bed," I said. "And Kate's mom sings her a lullaby every night. What of it?" I was mad—burning, hopping, mega-mad, Diary. Wouldn't you be? I can't believe they had the nerve to act like I'm the one who's not mature.

Luckily, Fiona stuck up for me. She said, "You guys call yourselves Lindsey's friends? That's way uncool what you did. You should apologize."

"Wait, Lindsey, I was just kidding," Bella said. "I'll show you the magazine."

"No, thanks," I answered. "I'm way too mature to roll around on the floor about some dumb magazine. You can just keep it to yourself." And then you know what I did, Diary? I walked away.

It felt good for about two seconds, until I started thinking again about what they said. I can't help it that I'm a few months younger. And yeah, I do have a doll collection that I play with sometimes. So what? I was starting to wish I lived in France, where friends probably always let friends play with dolls without making sneaky, snarky comments.

It's just that when they say stuff like that, I feel like something is happening. Something is changing. Maybe it's Kate and Bella who are changing, and I'll just stay the same old me. Maybe they won't want to be friends with me anymore, and it's starting already, like now, like today. This was just the first step. I won't have friends anymore, because the two of them will be off being different and more mature. They'll move to Hollywood and become famous actresses together. They'll discover the cure for cancer. They'll find a fossil of the oldest known human and get their pictures plastered all over *National Geographic*. And me? I'll be here plodding through fifth grade, too immature for words.

Okay, Diary. I just re-read what I wrote. It made me laugh a little. Just a little. Maybe they were just being jerks today, I dunno. I'm going to bed.

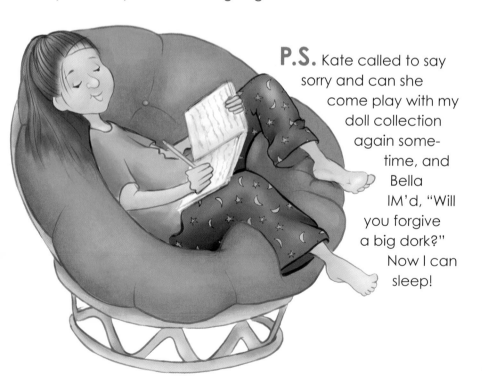

P.S. Kate called to say sorry and can she come play with my doll collection again some-time, and Bella IM'd, "Will you forgive a big dork?" Now I can sleep!

Girl Talk

1. Do best friends always have to be like each other or like the same things? What kinds of things do you have in common with your best friends? In what ways are you different from each other?

2. When you see your friends changing (liking new things and disliking old things), how does that make you feel? If change is a normal part of life, why does it feel so crummy sometimes?

3. Bella and Kate weren't very tactful in the way they pointed out Lindsey's differences. How could you and your friends talk about different interests and ideas without hurting each other's feelings?

4. Even best friends can sometimes say or do insensitive things. How do you let your friends know when they have crossed the line and hurt your feelings?

Chapter 7

Sometimes three can be four

or even more.

Big news: We're finally having the slumber party! Well, I'm not. Kate is. It's at her house. That's why Hailey is coming. She's mostly Kate's friend. Bella and I don't know her all that well.

"So are you sure you want to invite Hailey?" Bella asked. "Maybe she won't, like, want to do all the things we want to do."

"Like what kinds of things?" Kate asked, sounding exasperated.

"I don't know. You know, I mean, we like three chocolate cookies on top of bowls of mint chocolate chip ice cream. We like talking about the books we're reading and, like, suggesting new ones to each other. We like certain music and hate other kinds of music. Stuff like that." Bella shrugged.

"Uh, I know she likes ice cream, she reads books, and I'm guessing she likes some music and hates others, too. What's the big deal about Hailey? Fiona is coming, too."

"True," I said, jumping in. "But Fiona is Fiona. We've been in school with her since first grade. It's not like…." My voice trailed off.

"Like what, Lindsey? Like she's a threat or something?" Kate said.

Bella and I just looked at each other. It didn't really sound nice to say that about Fiona or Hailey either.

"You guys, come here and sit down," Kate said, pointing to her bed. "Look, I love you and I always will. But Hailey is nice and she's new to school. She needs friends. She's fun and I like her. Can you give her a chance?"

I nodded, sheepishly. Bella nodded.

"You know it's a rule at slumber parties that you have to have a good time, right?" Kate asked, grabbing her pillow. "Pillow fight!"

We were still laughing when Fiona and Hailey rang the doorbell together.

Hailey brought a bag of barbecue potato chips. "Crisps," she said, holding them out to Kate. Fiona brought a Magic Eight Ball. "So we can see the future," she said in her best spooky voice.

"I love that accent," I said. "Thanks," they both said at exactly the same time. We all laughed.

The rest of the night was a blast. We played ghost in the graveyard outside, and when Kate's mom said it was time to come in, we played our own version of name that tune. One person played a few notes of a song on Kate's keyboard, and everyone had to guess what it was.

"You're awesome at this," I said to Hailey. "I can't believe you got that Beatles song. That's, like, music my grandparents listened to."

My mom was right. It wasn't like Hailey was stealing Kate. She was just trying to be friends. With all of us.

And you know what? The party was the best ever! Having five people made it five times the fun.

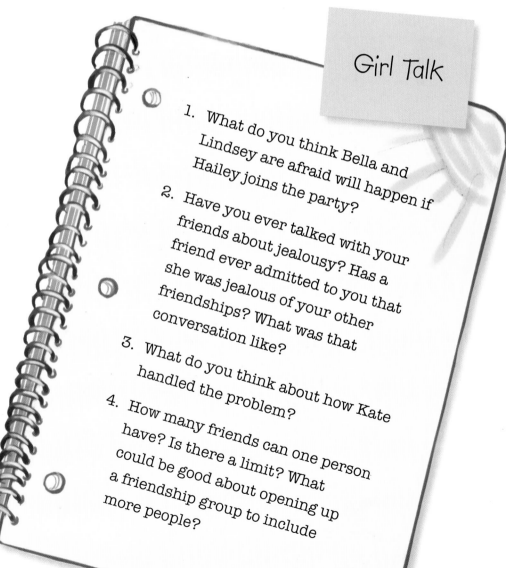

Girl Talk

1. What do you think Bella and Lindsey are afraid will happen if Hailey joins the party?

2. Have you ever talked with your friends about jealousy? Has a friend ever admitted to you that she was jealous of your other friendships? What was that conversation like?

3. What do you think about how Kate handled the problem?

4. How many friends can one person have? Is there a limit? What could be good about opening up a friendship group to include more people?

Most of the time, I love being part of a circle of three. Sometimes it can be hard, though. Like when Bella and I tell stories about our ballet class, and Kate doesn't know any of the people we're talking about. Or when Kate and Bella hang out together with their moms, and I feel really left out. When we fight, sometimes I think having two best friends is at least three times the trouble.

But nobody can tell jokes and make me laugh like Kate can. And no one else listens as well as Bella or comes up with such awesome ideas about what to do when we're bored. I like the things about them that make them different and cool in their own way.

Mom says that's how most things are, that the good part is totally worth the hard part, and I think she's right. Also, Kate and Bella and I have figured out some ways to make the hard parts not get too bad or last too long:

- Imagine how we would feel in **her** shoes.
- Try to include everyone, but don't lie if you can't.
- There are lots of things to do and lots of people to do them with.
- Ask ourselves if we're making too big a deal out of something.
- Don't ask a friend to choose between friends.
- Talk and listen to each other when there's a problem.
- Saying you're sorry may feel scary, but it brings friends back together, and that feels good.
- And probably the best thing we figured out is this:

Good things come in all sorts of numbers!